Three Paws and the Secret Cave

KAREN STRUCK

PAGE PUBLISHING, INC.
Conneaut Lake, PA

First originally published by Page Publishing 2021

ISBN 978-1-6624-0747-5 (pbk)
ISBN 978-1-6624-0749-9 (hc)
ISBN 978-1-6624-0748-2 (digital)

Printed in the United States of America

To those we have loved and lost...

Boots, the grizzly bear, and Cappy, the elderly mountain goat, are best friends although they did not start off as friends.

Two years ago, Cappy lost his footing and rolled down the side of a mountain. He was injured and asked Boots to help him. Boots agreed to help Cappy. In return, Cappy taught Boots how to catch salmon with only three paws when no one else believed in him.

Cyrus, king of the eagles, soared through the sky. He swooped down and landed beside Boots and friends. "Scarlet needs your help!" he said urgently. "She has not seen her grandfather, Cappy, in two days."

They all exchanged glances.

"Let's visit Scarlet on the mountaintop," Boots insisted. "Cyrus, can you send out a search party?"

Cyrus nodded and took off like a jet.

The green, grassy mountain was speckled with low-growing shrubs.

A herd of mountain goats nibbled on the grass and shrubs while Scarlet paced back and forth, searching for signs of her grandfather.

Scarlet spotted Boots and raced to his side. "Please help me find my grandfather!" she pleaded. "He hasn't been feeling well, and now he's disappeared."

Scarlet spent every day with her grandfather. He taught her about the joys of being a mountain goat and the love of nature like the bald eagle, the black-tailed deer, and the caribou. Cappy would always remind her to keep her heart open to new adventures and to new friends.

Cyrus and his son, Blizzard, descended toward the herd and hovered above Scarlet. "We found your grandfather, Scarlet!" Cyrus announced.

"We saw him grazing on grass about an hour's walk from here. He disappeared into a small cave."

Scarlet shrieked with delight! "Oh Cyrus, please guide us to the cave."

Cyrus and Blizzard led the entire herd to Cappy's secret cave.

"Why would he leave without saying goodbye?" Chinook asked as she walked beside Sockeye.

Pepe straddled Scarlet's neck as if he were riding on a horse. He hugged Scarlet and said, "We will find out soon enough."

Cappy was a well-respected goat who had been a mentor, or teacher, to the younger goats. His absence was felt from the entire herd.

As they approached the cave, Cappy appeared at the opening, surprised but very happy. He was immediately surrounded by his many friends. Tears filled his eyes as he felt the love of all who came to see him.

Scarlet approached her grandfather. "Grandcappy, why did you leave?"

Cappy nuzzled his head against Scarlet's head. "Dear Scarlet, you know I have not been well."

Scarlet did not want to believe her grandfather's journey was coming to an end.

"I have lived a long and very happy life, but it will soon be time for me to join our ancestors in goat heaven."

"I know that, Grandcappy," Scarlet said. "But why would you want to be *alone* at this time?"

Cyrus, Blizzard, Boots, Sockeye, Chinook, Pepe, and Scarlet formed a semicircle in front of the herd, eagerly awaiting Cappy's answer.

He paused for a moment, noticing more and more wildlife friends joining the group. "I am not as strong as I used to be, and I can no longer defend myself against predators." He smiled at Scarlet and continued, "I found this secret cave where I can rest in peace as I am very weak and very tired."

Scarlet faced her friends and the herd with an attitude of optimism.

She spoke loud and clear, exclaiming, "It is time to celebrate my grandfather's life. Let the celebration begin!"

"Vamos de fiesta!" (Let's party!) Pepe shouted.

All the animals chatted excitedly, visiting with one another.

Everyone shared stories about Cappy.

Boots' had one lingering question for Cappy. "Remember two years ago when we met, you told me you had friends in high places who owed you a favor?"

"Yes, I remember," replied Cappy.

"You were referring to the eagles. Why would eagles owe you a favor?" Boots asked.

Cappy sat on the grass, recalling the day he first met Cyrus.

"It was a beautiful spring day, like today, when I noticed a young eagle flying overhead. A large eagle appeared, unexpectedly, and started to nip at the wing of the younger eagle. That big eagle was being a bully.

The young eagle slowly fell from the sky. I shouted, '*Pinwheel formation*!' and ten goats made a circle with our bottoms, touching, heads facing outward. The young eagle, *Blizzard*, landed on our fluffy backs."

Blizzard hugged Cappy. "You saved me," Blizzard said.

Cyrus joined them. "I told Cappy I owed him a big favor, and that favor was granted when you and the bears enjoyed your salmon feast two years ago."

"What a story!" Boots laughed.

Everyone nodded.

Cappy saw the sun setting and knew his time was near. "Thank you for this celebration of life," he said gratefully as he faced the crowd of friends before him. "I am honored to have been a part of your lives."

Every animal stood silent and bowed their heads.

Scarlet escorted her grandfather into the cave. Forget-me-not flowers in shades of pink and purple covered the ground like a colorful carpet.

Cappy laid on his left side. Scarlet laid on her right side, mirroring her grandfather. Her nose touched his.

"I will stay until you take your last breath," Scarlet whispered. "I love you, Grandcappy."

He kissed her nose. "When the stars twinkle at night, know that I will be waving to you. I will always be with you...in your heart."

As the sky grew dark, Scarlet could see the twinkling stars above. It made her smile. Her grandfather was at peace.

Scarlet joined her friends.

They each held a forget-me-not flower in the palm of their hand, raised their hands toward the sky, and cheered, "To Cappy!"

The End

About the Author

My daughter, Rachel, and Molly

Molly 8/1/95-4/16/17

Kaya & Lily

-We will meet again on the rainbow Bridge-

"Your life was a blessing,
your memory a treasure,
you are loved beyond words
and missed beyond measure"

Garrett Paul

Death is a natural part of the human experience. Three Paws and the Secret Cave serves to prepare young people and adults alike, in dealing with a "timely" and anticipated death following a chronic illness. Scarlet, the young and intuitive mountain goat, must come to terms with the passing of her beloved grandfather. Sometimes sick animals may be unable to keep up with their herd. In their weakened condition, they are unable to protect themselves and must hide, alone, to avoid predators. Animals do feel grief and practice their own grieving rituals. Scarlet, Boots and friends show Cappy how much he is loved and honored by celebrating his life while he is alive. Named after the constellation, Capricornus, Cappy reassures Scarlet that he will be waving to her as the stars twinkle above. His spirit lives on in her heart.

Memories of our loved ones become our treasure, our peace, and our comfort.